Sally

the
COMET

To Trent,
Enjoy.
Zooming
through
space
with Sally!

Karen Deming

Written by **Anna Courie**

Illustrated by **Karen Deming**

Copyright 2014   All rights reserved

Once upon a time
there was a comet named Sally.
She was a very sad and lonely comet.

She felt she had no friends as she orbited the solar system.

Fun Fact
Comets are made
of dust and ice which
break off and reflect
the Sun's rays. These
shining pieces are
what make a comet's
tail appear to glow.

One day, Sally the Comet was passing by the Sun.

"Oh Sun, I am so lonely. I have no friends who fly with me on my trips around the solar system. What ever will I do? It makes me so sad to be lonely."

"Sally, Sally," said the Sun, "you are not alone in the solar system."

Fun Fact

The Sun is really a star at the center of our solar system. It appears large to us because it is closer than any other star.

There are planets and asteroids, comets, and moons all in the solar system and I bet they all want to be your friend! You just have to stop and talk to them!"

Fun Fact

The solar system is the Sun and all of the objects in space that orbit the Sun.

"Oh Sun! What a wonderful idea you have," exclaimed Sally.

"I will have to call out to the planets as I pass them in my orbit. I will start with Mercury."

Fun Fact
An orbit is the path an object takes as it circles around another object in space.

"Excellent idea, Sally," replied the Sun. "Make sure you tell me of all your new friends when you come to see me next!"

Sally zoomed off on her orbit to the planet Mercury.

Fun Fact

Mercury travels around the Sun in only 88 days. This is the shortest orbit in our solar system.

Mercury is the smallest planet
in the solar system and at first
Sally couldn't find Mercury.

"Oh Mercury!
Where are you?
I am Sally the Comet
and I want to
be your friend."

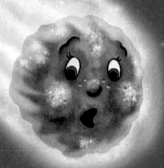

Fun Fact

Mercury is
36 million
miles away
from the Sun.

"Hello Sally! I am so happy that you stopped to talk to me. I am not as beautiful as Neptune's blue haze, or as fascinating as Saturn's rings or as big as Jupiter.

I sometimes think people forget me because I am so small. You have made my day! Thank you for talking to me."

Fun Fact
Mercury has more craters than any other planet in our solar system.

"Mercury, I am so delighted that you talked to me. I am made mostly of ice and dirt, so your warmth from the sun makes me happy.

I think you are a beautiful planet. I am glad we will be friends. I will be sure to stop every time I come by on my orbit," said Sally.

Fun Fact
Mercury doesn't have an atmosphere, which allows heat to escape its surface.

"Cheerio, Sally! I will see you when you come back!"

And so Sally flew off to see Venus next. Sally was sure she would love Venus since she is named for the Roman god of love.

Fun Fact

Mercury is made mostly of iron.

When Sally got to Venus, she was very stormy, dusty, and cloudy. Sally wasn't sure what to say.

Timidly, Sally called out, "Hello, Venus. My name is Sally the Comet and I am trying to make friends in the solar system. Would you like to be friends?"

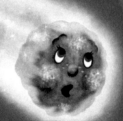

"Hello, Sally," replied Venus, "if you are not afraid of my heat and clouds, I will be happy to be your friend."

Fun Fact
Even though Mercury is closer to the Sun, Venus is the hottest planet in the solar system because of its dense atmosphere.

"We should go shopping together. I am thinking about getting some rings like Saturn to compete in the Miss Universe pageant. What do you think?"

Fun Fact

A comet's tail can be several million miles long.

"Oh that would be so fun! I wonder what I can collect to make my tail so many pretty colors? I wouldn't want to compete against you though, Venus. You are now my friend. I will be sure to come see you though."

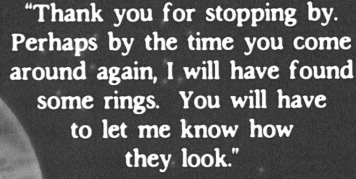

"Thank you for stopping by. Perhaps by the time you come around again, I will have found some rings. You will have to let me know how they look."

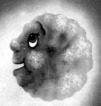

"Bye, Venus! Until next time," said Sally. And off went Sally to see Earth.

Fun Fact

Some planetary rings are dust, which may have been caused by meteor impacts on a planet's moons.

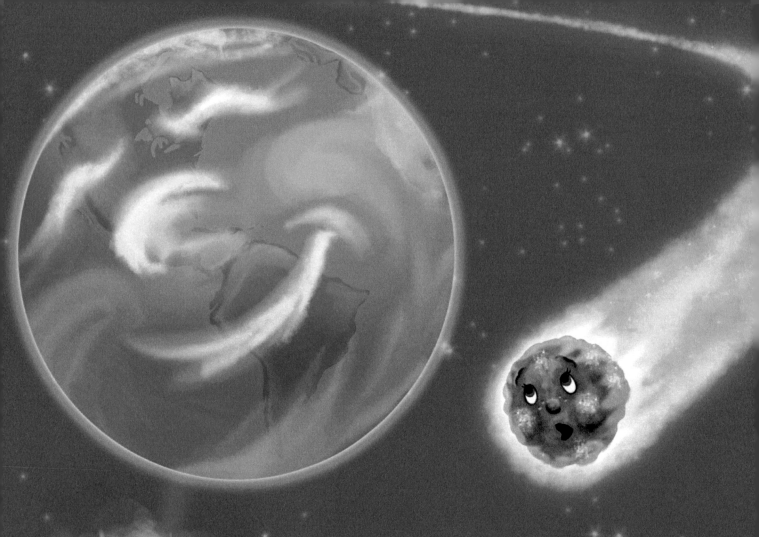

Fun Fact

The Earth is wider around the equator than it is from pole to pole. Its squat shape is called an ellipsoid.

Earth is so amazing when you fly by.
The blue of the oceans and the white
of the clouds and the brown of
the earth sparkles from space
like the most amazing
creation in the universe.
Sally was in awe flying by Earth.

"Hello, Earth. My name is Sally the Comet and I am looking for new friends in the solar system. I am meeting all the planets.

Will you be my friend?"

"Hello, Sally! I hope you will be my friend too. I have lots of friends. They are called people, animals, trees, and fish. They all live on me."

Fun Fact

The Earth rotates every 24 hours which gives us our days and nights.

"The people on earth get very excited to see comets in the night sky, so every time you come to see me, you will also have many friends on my surface. In fact they will probably have 'Sally the Comet' parties!'"

"Oh how delightful! I love a party," said Sally. "If I pick up lots of dust and ice on my orbit, I can make many streaks through the sky. I will be sure to fly by slowly in your area so that the people of Earth will be delighted by my tail. I will glow pink with pleasure."

Fun Fact

Some comets can pass by Earth every 20 years. Other comets can take as long as 200 years between visits, while some fly by once and never return again.

"Wonderful!" said Earth, "Come back soon. Don't stay away for 76 years like Halley the Comet."

"Ok, Earth. Bye! See you soon," said Sally.

Sally was fairly bursting with excitement from all the friends she was meeting on her travels. The solar system never seemed so big.

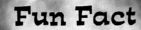

Fun Fact

Halley's Comet is the most famous comet. It last passed by Earth in 1986. Its next visit will be in 2061!

She was excited to be off to Mars, but a little scared too.
Mars is named after the Roman god of war.
She did not want to get hurt.

"Hello, Mars!   How are you today?
I am Sally the Comet," she said.

"Grummmph," said Mars.

"What was that?" asked Sally.

Fun Fact
Mars is the
second
smallest
planet in the
solar system.

"Grmmmmphhhh! I am grumpy and I'm usually angry and red. But I still would like a friend. I might just grump at you a lot," said Mars.

"Sometimes people who are grumpy need friends most of all," said Sally.

"I will be your friend anyway and maybe over my trips to visit, you will get less grumpy."

Fun Fact

Mars has many volcanoes including the largest volcano in the solar system.

"Grmmmphfff," said Mars. "Ok. See you next time. Grmmmphfff."

Sally took off zooming through the asteroid belt going here and there so as not to collide with one of the big rocks! Some were so big they could be moons! Sally was going to get through it though, she was so excited to talk to Jupiter.

With a hop, skip, and a jump, Sally took off for Jupiter. Jupiter is the largest planet in the solar system. Sally was a little afraid of feeling small

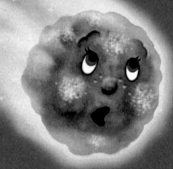

Fun Fact
Ceres is the largest known asteroid. It is about 568 miles across and can be found between Mars and Jupiter.

and insignificant next to Jupiter. She remembered that Mercury felt that way too next to the sun and thought, "I am just myself. I am a part of the solar system just like Jupiter and Mercury. I am just different."

Flying up to the Great Red Spot, Sally stared straight at Jupiter's unique eye and said, "Good morning, Jupiter! I am here to be your friend." With a yawn and a stretch, Jupiter's gases swirled a little and it looked like the spot opened just a bit to look sleepily at Sally.

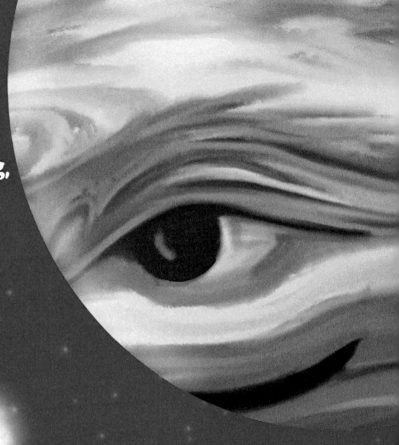

"Well good morning, young comet. Welcome to this part of the universe. You are entering the gas planets and we are very big because we have lots of space between our molecules. We also have a lot of energy since all of our gases move around in us."

Fun Fact
Jupiter's Great Red Spot is really a giant storm that is 12,400 miles long and 7,500 miles wide.

Sally tried to look at Jupiter through one eye to pretend she was a little Jupiter. "How fascintating, Jupiter. You are so magnificent in your greatness. I love your Great Red Spot and how it winks at me! I think we are going to be very good friends."

Fun Fact

Jupiter is the largest planet in our solar system. It is more than one thousand times larger than Earth.

"Thank you for visiting me, Sally. I think I shall go back to sleep. It's very dark and cold this far from the sun and sometimes a nap is just the thing."

From Jupiter, Sally flew off to Saturn. She thought Saturn was the most amazing planet of them all with his rings, but she was also learning that all the planets were unique and amazing with all their own personalities.

"Hello Saturn. I am Sally the Comet and I am meeting new friends. Would you like to be friends? I have always thought your rings were amazing."

"Why hullooo, Sally! Why don't you come take a whirl around my rings? You can pretend I am a roller coaster. I will make my rings spin faster and faster for your ride."

Fun Fact
Saturn's rings are made up of dust, ice, and rocks.

Sally giggled. How fun. Not only was Saturn pretty, but he could do tricks too. Sally rode Saturn's rings round and round.

"WHEEEEEEEEEEEEEEE!" she cried!

Fun Fact

It takes over 29 years for Saturn to orbit the sun once.

"That was so much fun. I cannot wait to come back by and do that again."

"I would love for you to come back," said Saturn, "and you can always ride my rings. Have a super trip. Bye!"

After leaving Saturn, Sally flew off to Uranus. When she got there, she realized that Uranus looked a little funny. Sally decided to fly sideways and all of a sudden Uranus looked right.

"Hello, Uranus. I am Sally the Comet and I want to be your friend. I see that you are a little different too!"

Fun Fact
Uranus is the only planet in our solar system to rotate on its side. Scientists believe that a small moon-sized object hit Uranus, but no one knows for certain.

"I think it's so fun that you orbit different from the other planets. And you have little rings too! Maybe I will get rings one day as well."

Fun Fact
Uranus has 27 moons that we know about. The largest moon is called Titania.

"Hi Sally! Yes, I like to look at the solar system from a different perspective. When I bumped into a moon a long time ago, it sat me on my side and I have turned this way ever since. It's fun to march to my own tune."

"Perhaps next time, you will change your orbit and come around the solar system a different way. You never know what you will learn when you look at things differently," said Uranus.

"I will have to do that. Until next time though. I am getting dizzy," Sally giggled, as she straightened herself out.

Fun Fact
Uranus doesn't really have rings that turn into a curl on its top, but wouldn't that be fun?

As Sally flew off to Neptune, she could see this blue glow in the distance. Neptune was named for the Roman god of the ocean and it did look like a ball of water in the far off distance. It made Sally want to go for a swim.

"Hello Neptune. I am Sally the Comet and I want to be your friend."

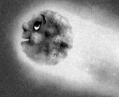

Fun Fact

Neptune has 14 moons that we know about. Because Neptune is so far away, it may even have more that we haven't discovered yet.

"Well hello, Sally. Why don't you stop and have a spot of tea with me! It may be a little frozen since we are so far from the sun and I am icy cold, but I would love to visit with you," said Neptune.

So, Sally sat for a bit, visiting Neptune, and they had tea. It was delightful. Neptune even made blue snow cones to share, although Neptune's strong winds almost blew the snow cones away.

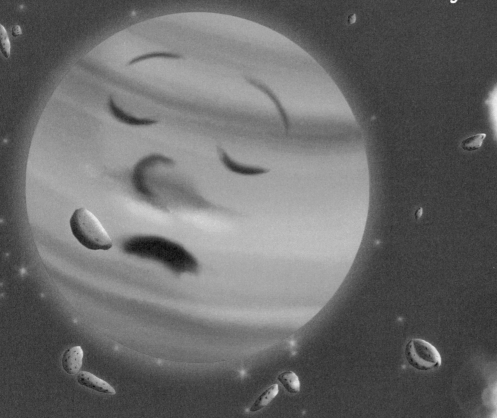

"Thank you for your hospitality, Neptune. We will have to have another tea party in the solar system. I will be sure to stop by again."

Fun Fact
Neptune's moons aren't all round like our moon. Some are shaped like cones and some moons even look a little like cups.

So Sally flew off to visit Pluto.
She had to fly off course since Pluto orbits
the solar system on a different path.

Fun Fact

Pluto has at
least five moons,
but more may be
discovered in 2015
when the New
Horizons space
probe visits
Pluto.

When Sally arrived at Pluto,
he was crying.
"WAHHHHHHHHHHH,
boooooo hoooooo, I am
so sad!"

"Whatever is wrong?"
asked Sally.

"I used to be a planet, but now
they call me a dwarf and some
people call me a Planetoid!
Oh the names! They wound me!
I so enjoyed being the littlest planet
in the solar system and now I am
just a random rock!
WAHHHHHHHHHHHHHH."

Fun Fact

Pluto is about
two-thirds the
size of our
moon.

"They may change their mind again and give me another name! Next I could be a moon!" he cried.

Fun Fact

Pluto was said to be the smallest planet in our solar system for 76 years until it was decided that it was just one of many large objects in the Kuiper belt.

"Oh Pluto, it doesn't matter what you are! I will be your friend anyway. You can be a planet, or a dwarf planet, or an asteroid and you are still special. I will like you any way you are," said Sally.

Pluto sniffed. "Really, truly? You will love me anyway? This is the best news I have had since they took away my planet status."

Sniff, sigh... "WHAHHHHHH, I'm not a planet anymore! I am so sad!" Sniff, sniff... "But you promise to be my friend?"

"Yes," said Sally, "I will be your friend and I will always take time to visit you on my trip through the solar system if you will be my friend too."

Fun Fact

Pluto was found as a result of astronomer Percival Lowell's search for planets beyond Neptune. The Lowell Observatory in Arizona is named after him.

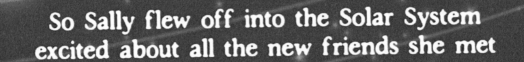

So Sally flew off into the Solar System excited about all the new friends she met

Fun Fact
Even though our solar system is really big, it is only a small part of the galaxy called "The Milky Way."

and how many great friends she will always be able to meet no matter where she is in her travels.

She realized that sometimes to make friends, she had to reach out...

and be a friend too.

Fun Fact
Sally is constantly moving through the solar system, but she learned that good friends are worth going the distance.

Made in the USA
San Bernardino, CA
18 March 2015